For Alex

First edition 2022

Library of Congress Catalog Card Number 2021953474
ISBN 978-1-5362-1566-3

22 23 24 25 26 27 CPG 10 9 8 7 6 5 4 3 2 1

Printed in A. Maung, Samutsakorn, Thailand

This book was typeset in Caslon 540.
The illustrations were created using watercolor and typographic artwork.

Candlewick Studio
an imprint of
Candlewick Press
99 Dover Street
Somerville, Massachusetts 02144

www.candlewickstudio.com

One & Everything

SAM WINSTON

CANDLEWICK STUDIO

an imprint of Candlewick Press

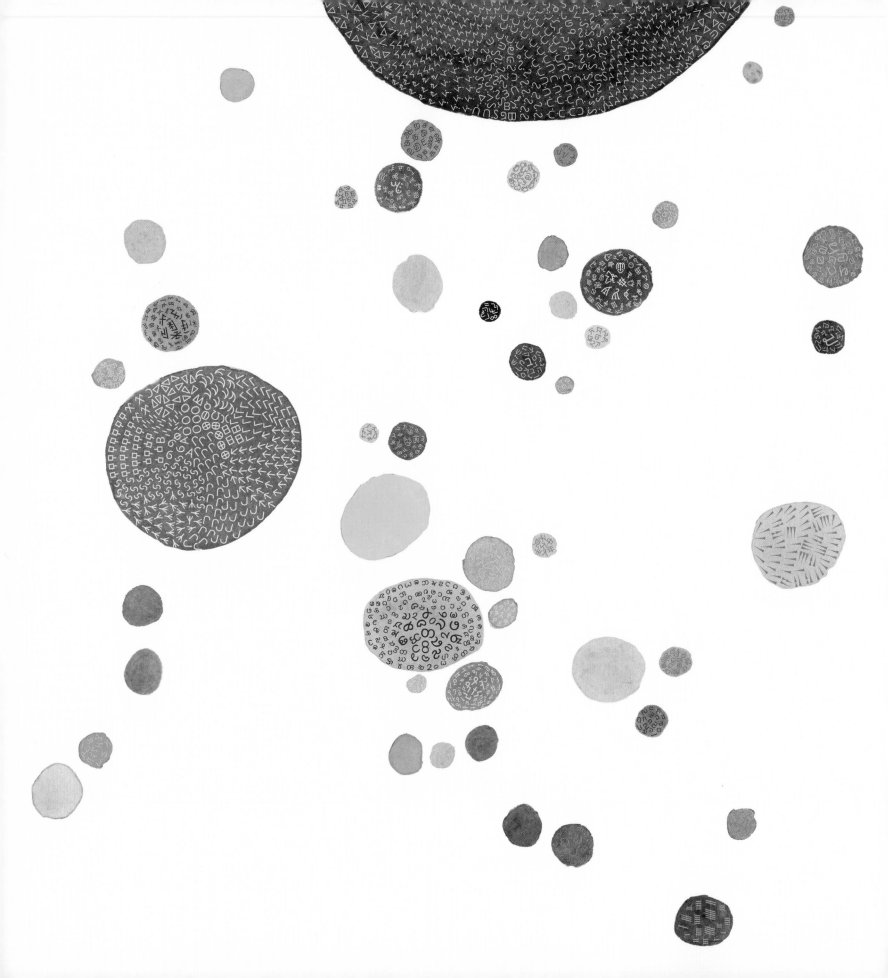

Once

there were many stories

for

the world.

Some

had beautiful

sunsets . . .

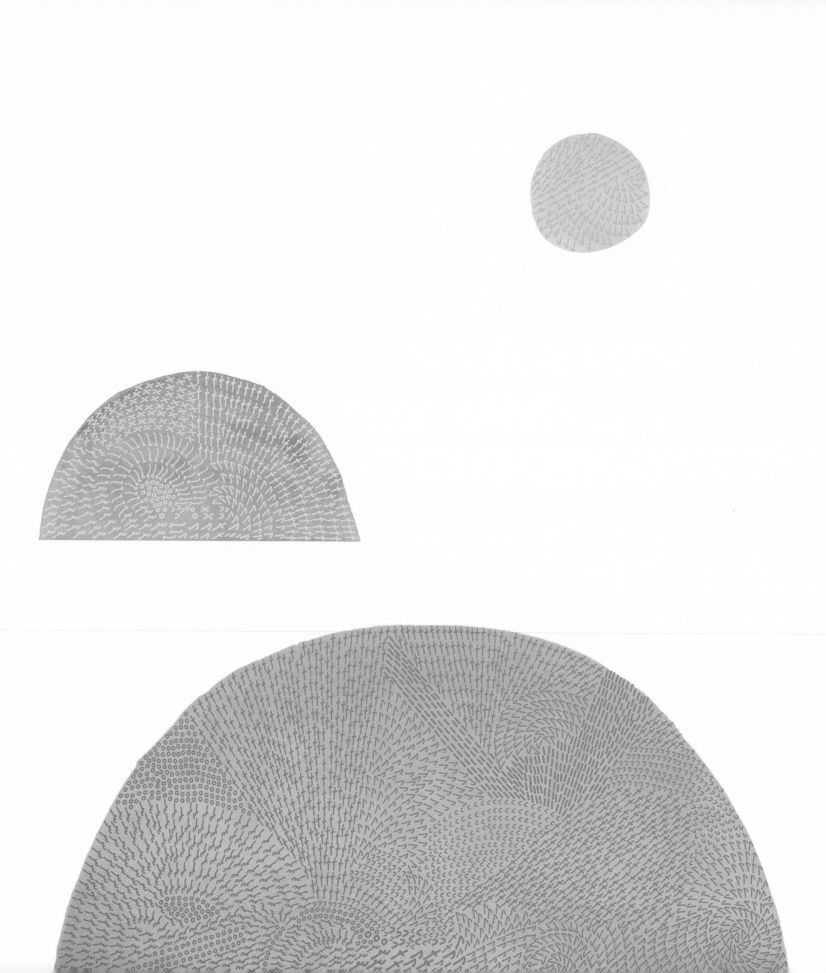

the sea . . .

at the bottom of

Others lived

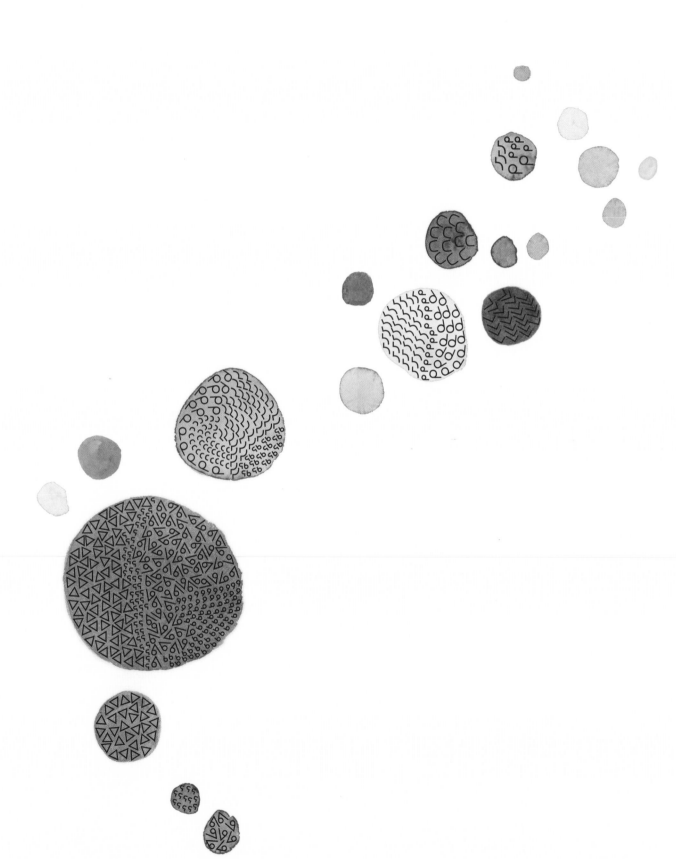

while others were simply full of dogs.

But there was one story that decided it was going to be — that perhaps it already was — the most important story in the world.

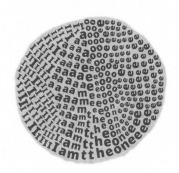

When this story approached another, older
story, instead of listening to it,

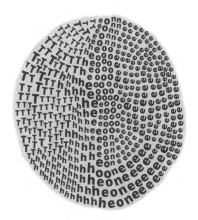 

this bold story said, "Actually, I am the
One, the Only story."

And it ate up the older story in one gulp.

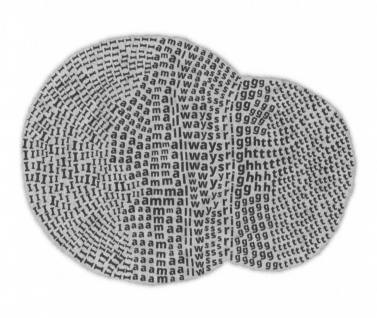

The One got very excited. Soon it came upon more stories—one with fairies, one with dinosaurs, and a really nice one with a funny song in it.

"I am the Only Story," it said, and with a giant slurp, all the others went down into its belly.

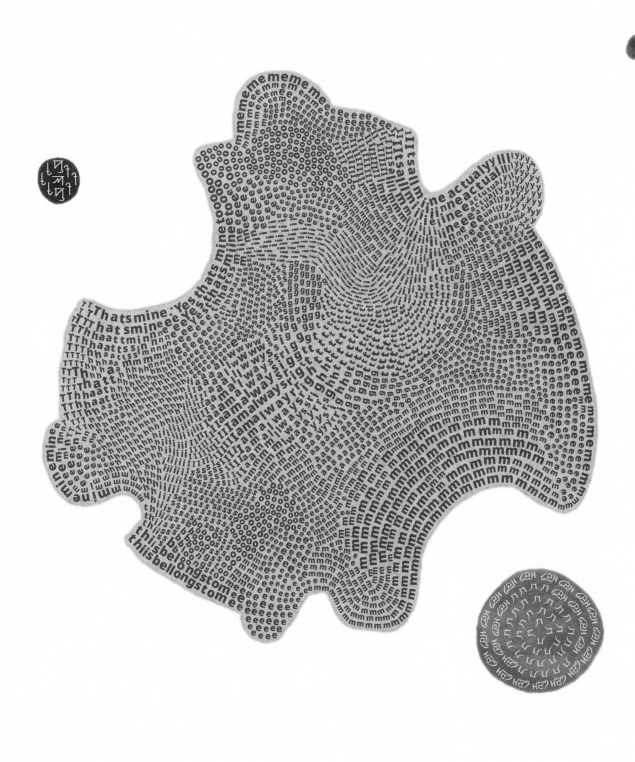

Before long, the One and Only story was
very nearly the last story in the world.
In fact, this storybook you are reading now
was probably the only other story left.

"Hey!" said the One. "I AM THE ONLY STORY."

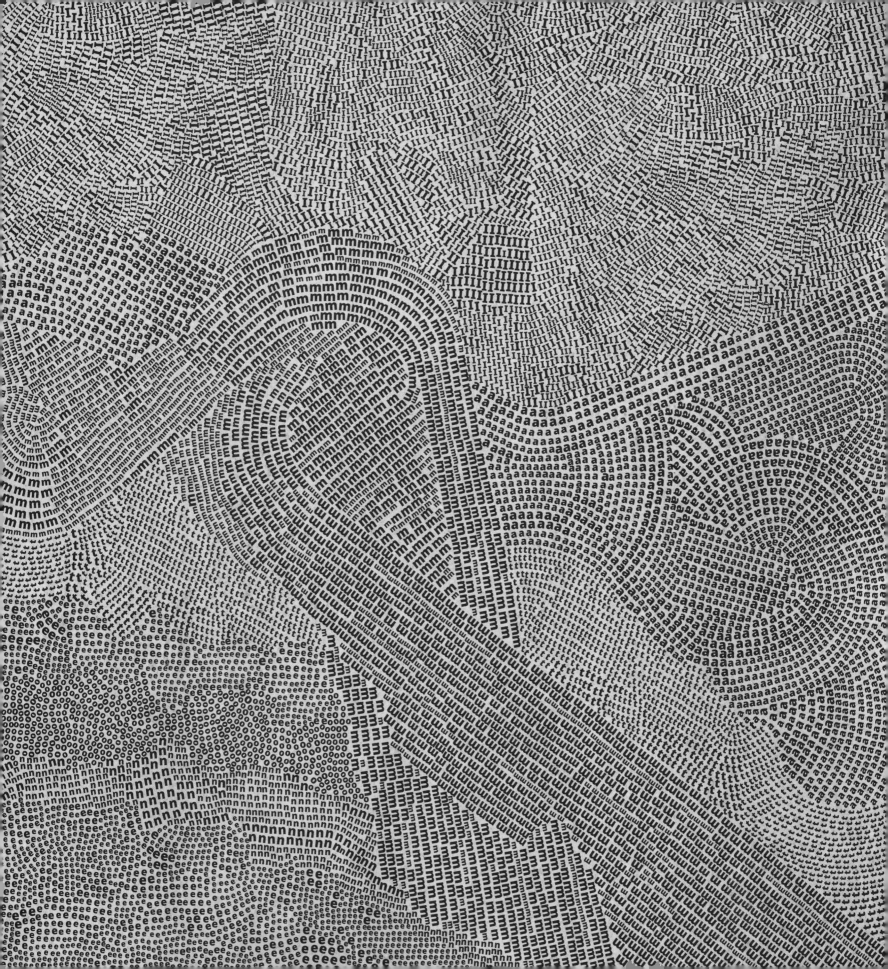

It was very dark inside the One,

so dark it was hard to tell if there were any pieces of the other stories left at all.

But inside the One's belly, something was
happening. A few letters got together, then
words. Soon there began to be whispers.
And then a voice spoke out loud.

"One," it said. "Can we ask you
something?"

"Of course," said the One.

"If you have eaten all the stories in the world, does that mean that somewhere in your belly you have the magic Ogham words?"

"Of course," said the One (thinking, *whatever those are*).

"Do you have every Adlam letter?"

"Indeed," said the One, feeling a little nervous.

"So actually, does that mean you have every word for every story ever told in you?"

"Why, yes, I do," said the One, proudly this time.

"Well," said the voice, "it seems to me that you're not the One Story then. You're Every Story!"

There was a long pause.

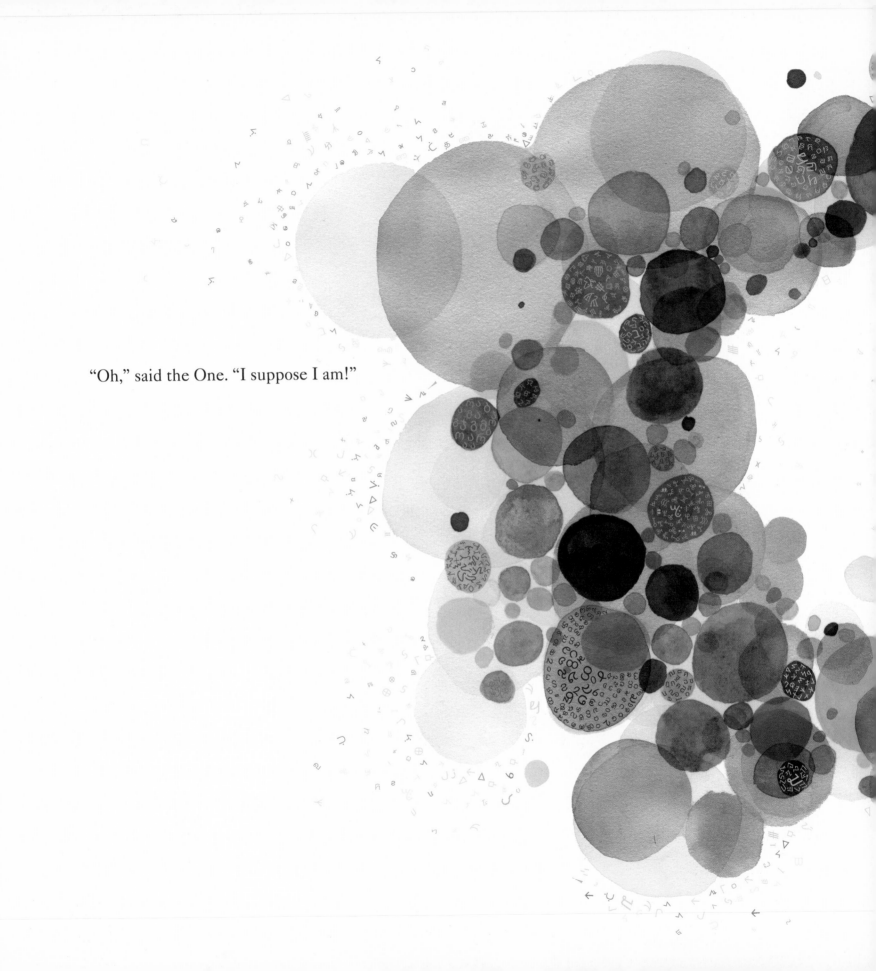

"Oh," said the One. "I suppose I am!"

And with that, the One exploded into every story imaginable.

And all that was left was a question.

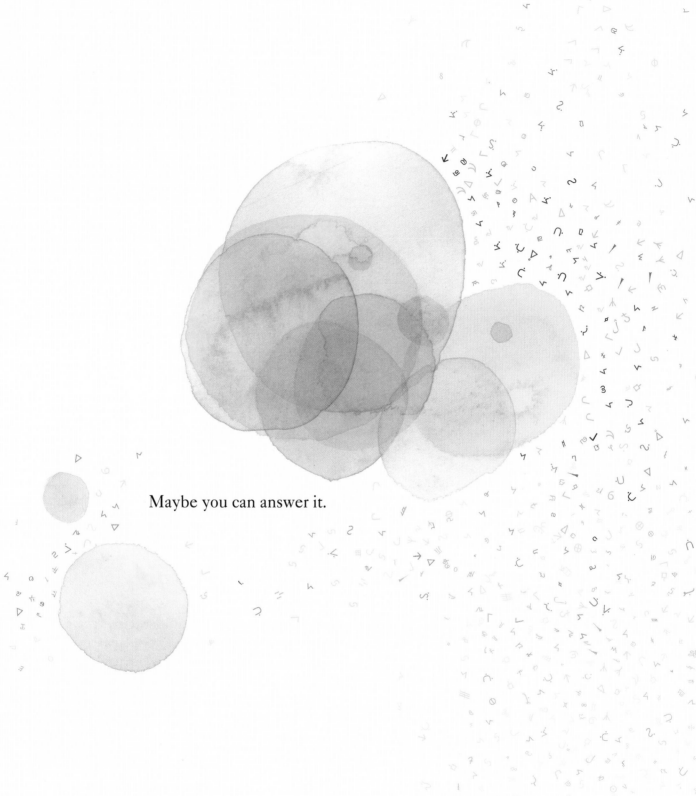

Maybe you can answer it.

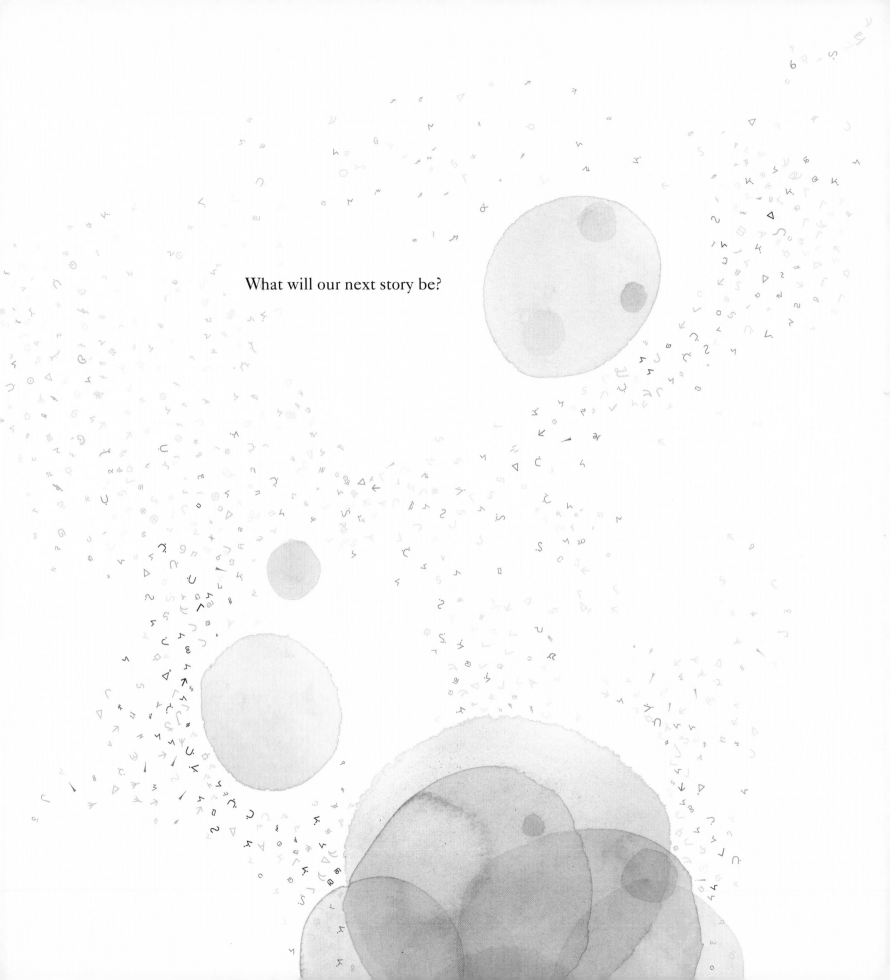

What will our next story be?

Author's Note

말이 씨가 된다. *A word becomes a seed.*
—*Korean proverb*

Writing is a few thousand years old, and if you were to measure that against how long humans have been using spoken language, then it can be considered a very new technology.

Even though we can't be sure when speech began, current estimates range from as late as fifty thousand years ago to as early as a few million years ago. Which means that we have been speaking at least forty-five thousand years longer than we have been writing.

A script is when someone captures how a language looks written down. One of the most common ways to do this is with an alphabet, where marks represent certain sounds. We are very inventive in our mark making, and we now have hundreds of different alphabets and scripts (some of which appear in this book).

We are also very creative about how we write scripts, using all sorts of different materials. There's probably not much we haven't tried drawing on: wood, mud, metal, skin, and stone to name just a few. Nowadays we use mostly screens and paper to carry our words.

Right now, you're reading a living language (one that many people still use). In this book we have living languages, languages that are no longer used, and even languages that no one can remember the meaning of.

We think there are currently more than seven thousand languages in the world, spoken by around eight billion people. It's hard to know exactly how many languages there are because words change over time and can drift into other languages. Languages, like people, do not sit still.

With the Information Age has come a rapid shift in how we live. Ideas, goods, and conversations circulate the world like never before. These changes have put a lot of pressure on us to speak the same language. Today it's believed that more than half the world's population speaks one of only twenty-three languages from the thousands in existence.

This growth in a few global languages has resulted in the loss of many other languages, the speed of which is accelerating as the world becomes more connected. Half of the world's languages are now under threat of disappearing.

Once a language is gone, it's hard to find out what its speakers knew and thought and how they lived. Their narratives, stories, and fables become lost. This is why communities and organizations have started to record their languages and create programs to teach new speakers. But the growth of these new projects cannot keep up with the rate of language loss across our planet.

Language is a unique expression of what it is to be human, and the more words and languages we have, the richer and more diverse our world is. Maintaining and honoring the beautiful old stories and creating new narratives are at the heart of a language's survival. With a new generation of story keepers and creators, we could see many of these languages flourish.

Some Characters to Be Found in *One & Everything*

Thaana

Sunset page

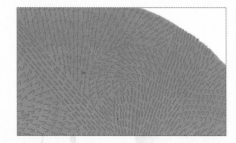

Thaana is the script for Dhivehi (or Maldivian), the language spoken in the Maldives, an island nation in the Indian Ocean. Many of the letters are based on numbers and have a unique alphabetical order. Words run from right to left, perhaps originally as a way to keep the script's meanings more secret and harder to learn (the script that existed when Thaana was invented ran from left to right and was eventually replaced by Thaana). Another theory is that Thaana was invented so that Arabic words, which also run right to left, could be translated and read by people in the Maldives.

The Maldives has a long tradition of tales of fantastic sea creatures and great ocean voyages. With more than a thousand coral islands, it is a land of beaches, palm trees, and ocean sunrises and sunsets. In *One & Everything* the words for sunrise (﷽), sunset (﷽), and sun (﷽) appear.

Canadian Aboriginal Syllabics

Sea page

The Canadian Aboriginal Syllabics were developed in the 1840s as a written system for the oral Ojibwe and Cree languages. They were later adapted for Inuktitut, the language of the Inuit people, and for several Athabascan languages of the Northwest, including Slave, Dogrib, and Chipewyan, and inspired the Carrier Syllabics, created in 1885. The letter shapes are uniquely designed to rotate. Rotating a consonant symbol ninety degrees changes the following vowel.

In *One & Everything* the words for whale (ᐅᒡᕕ), ringed seal (ᓇᑦᓯᖅ), and Sedna (ᓴᐁᓇ) appear. In Inuit mythology, Sedna is the goddess of the sea. When her father tried to throw her overboard, she clung to the boat, but he cut her loose by chopping off her fingers. As she sank to the bottom, her fingers turned into seals, walruses, and whales—all of which the Inuit hunt and depend on for food—and thus she became the mother of the ocean.

Egyptian Hieroglyphs

Dogs page

Egyptian hieroglyphs were used for writing in ancient Egypt as many as five thousand years ago and are one of the oldest forms of writing. Unlike most modern alphabets, hieroglyphs use pictorial elements to represent objects, ideas, and sounds.

The characters were engraved or painted on clay, stone, or papyrus, a paper made from reeds that grew plentifully along the banks of the Nile.

In *One & Everything* the hieroglyphs ⟨symbols⟩ all appear. Described as a dog, jackal, or wolf, canines were worshipped and sometimes even buried next to the pharaohs in their tombs.

The two best-known Egyptian gods associated with canines were Wepwawet and Anubis. Wepwawet was a wolf-headed god whose name means "opener of ways." He was connected to finding the right path, especially in war and during the soul's journey into the underworld. Jackal-headed Anubis, the other canine god, was one of the lords of the underworld.

Phaistos Disk

Old story page

In *One & Everything* the signs ⟨symbols⟩ are from the Phaistos Disk. The disk was found on the island of Crete in the Mediterranean and is thought to be more than 3,500 years old.

The disk was made by pushing different stamps into wet clay in a circular pattern and then baking the clay at a very high temperature. It is a good example of how the evolution of writing has involved many different experiments, with different peoples at various times writing on stone, bone, palm leaves, and even human skin as tattoos.

No one is entirely sure what the inscriptions on the Phaistos Disk mean. It remains a challenge and a mystery that fascinates us to this day.

Tibetan

Slurp page

The Tibetan script is used wherever Tibetan people are to be found—not only in Tibet but also across China, South Asia, and many Western societies. It is closely linked to Tibetan Buddhism and is often seen on prayer flags, prayer wheels, and Buddhist documents. It is also widely used for calligraphy and in art.

The Tibetan script is commonly used for textbooks, storybooks, and many types of literature, including history, autobiography, poems, and medical texts.

One & Everything includes the Tibetan word ཀླུང (lung), which has a variety of meanings. It can mean "wind" but also refers to inhalation and exhalation, and even to the concept of what type of energy we have in our bodies.

Cuneiform

Slurp page

Cuneiform, one of the oldest known forms of writing in the world, was used to write several languages in what is now the Middle East. It developed from pictographic symbols engraved in clay and was adapted using wedge-shaped impressions to express increasingly complex ideas.

In *One & Everything* the cuneiform marks 𒁹 𒈫 𒐈 𒑀 𒐊 𒑂 are the numbers one to six. The Sumerian counting system was based on cycles of sixty, which over time fell out of use and was replaced by how we count today, using cycles of ten. One of the areas in which we still use cycles of sixty (called sexagesimal) and its factors is how we measure time. We use Sumerian counting in measuring our minutes, hours, and days.

Syloti

Slurp page

In *One & Everything* the letters পুথী spell the word *puthi*, pronounced like *futi* in the Syloti/Sylheti language. Puthis are written poems in the form of a book that are sung or chanted to listeners. The melodic recitation of puthis had been a traditional way for elders to pass on stories and lessons to people in the community who didn't read.

Syloti, or Sylheti or Siloti, is the language spoken on both sides of the border in northeastern Bangladesh and in southern Assam, India. National interests in Bangladesh became so strong in promoting Bangla, or Bengali, that it pushed aside many local and regional languages, including Syloti.

Syloti is now an example of how languages and their letters can travel the globe. The traditional Syloti Nagri script is endangered in its homeland because of political pressures but finds support from the Syloti/Sylheti community in the United Kingdom, a country halfway around the world, which has created many projects celebrating this language.

Ogham

Voice speaks pages

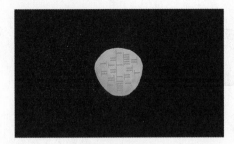

Ogham is an ancient Irish alphabet that was invented in about the fourth century CE and used in short messages carved on wooden sticks. It was later used for inscriptions on stone monuments and everyday objects, and it is occasionally found in the margins of medieval manuscripts for jokes, secrets, and even spells. Knowledge of the script was never entirely forgotten.

Ogham is a highly unusual writing system. All the letters are bundles of short strokes placed to one side or the other of a central stem line. Sometimes the stem line is the edge of a stone, in which case the letters are written in 3-D—a unique feature!

Traditionally ogham was written vertically—reading an ogham was said to be like climbing a tree, branch by branch. Each of the letters in the ogham alphabet has a name. Many are named after trees, and the letters ᚏᚈᚈᚏ, ᚈ, and ᚔᚔ (O, B, and D) in *One & Everything* are named onn, beith, and dair, the early Irish names for ash, birch, and oak.

Adlam

Ogham and Adlam page

The letters 𞤃, 𞤂, 𞤁, and 𞤀 in *One & Everything* (translating into English as M, L, D, and A) are the first four letters of the script known as Adlam, which is read from right to left. This recently invented script is used in Guinea and other countries in West Africa. The Adlam alphabet gets its name from these letters, which stand for Alkule Dandayɗe Leñol Mulugol, meaning "the alphabet that protects the people from vanishing."

Adlam was invented in 1989 by two brothers, Abdoulaye and Ibrahima Barry, who decided that their language, Fulani, needed its own alphabet. They were still in school at the time, but that didn't stop them from sketching symbols they thought would work. Adlam is remarkable both for the ages of its inventors and for the speed at which it moved from a handwritten local script to one that is now used on phones and computers around the world.

Cherokee

Explode pages

In *One & Everything* the letters ᏍᏓᎥᎠ spell the name Sequoyah. Sequoyah was a Cherokee who recognized the value of writing and set about making a modified syllabary for his people. He persisted for well over a decade, despite being ridiculed by many of his friends. One person who didn't tease him was his daughter Ayoka, who helped him over the years and became the first Cherokee to be able to read in her own language.

When he presented the finished script to the tribal council, they were not convinced. They gave the father and daughter a test. They separated the two and gave each of them dictation to see if the other could read it. And they were both successful! After seeing the script's worth, the council immediately gave orders that it should be taught, and within a few years the Cherokee were some of the most literate people in America.

When giant redwoods, a previously unknown species of tree, were identified by botanists in the mid-nineteenth century, the name *Sequoia gigantea* was ultimately given to them in honor of the Cherokee leader and his amazing achievement.

Where the Scripts Used in *One & Everything* Come From

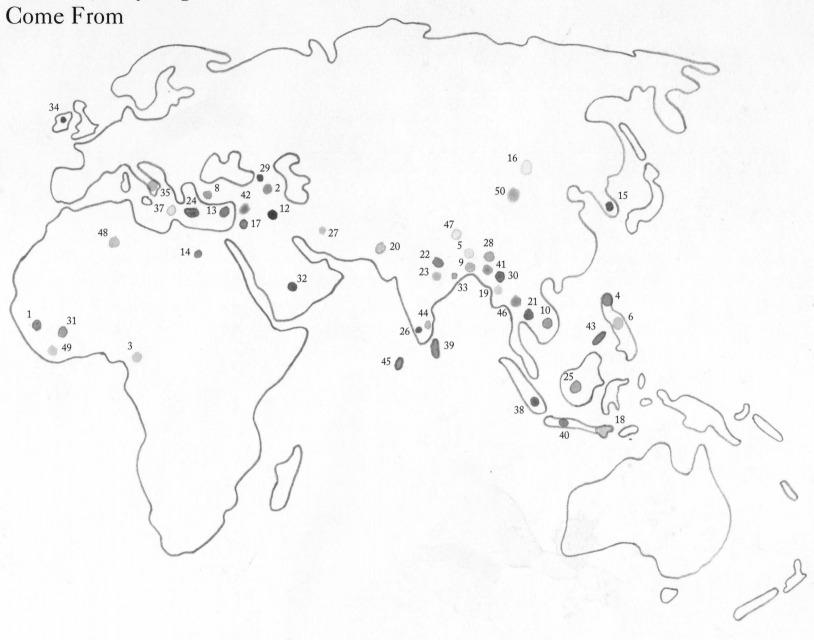

1	●	Adlam
2	●	Armenian
3	●	Bamum
4	●	Baybayin
5	●	Bengali
6	●	Buhid
7	●	Canadian Aboriginal Syllabics
8	●	Carian
9	●	Chakma
10	●	Cham

11	●	Cherokee
12	●	Cuneiform
13	●	Cypriot
14	●	Egyptian Hieroglyphs
15	●	Hangul
16	●	Hanzi
17	●	Hebrew
18	●	Javanese
19	●	Kayah Li
20	●	Kharosthi

21	●	Lanna
22	●	Lepcha
23	●	Limbu
24	●	Linear B
25	●	Lontara
26	●	Malayalam
27	●	Mandaic
28	●	Meitei Mayek
29	●	Mkhedruli
30	●	Myanmar

31	●	N'Ko
32	●	Naskh
33	●	Odia
34	●	Ogham
35	●	Old Italic
36	●	Osage
37	●	Phaistos Disk
38	●	Rejang
39	●	Sinhala
40	●	Sundanese

41	●	Syloti
42	●	Syriac
43	●	Tagbanwa
44	●	Tamil
45	●	Thaana
46	●	Thai
47	●	Tibetan
48	●	Tifinagh
49	●	Vai
50	●	Yi

One thing to note when looking at this map is that an alphabet is not a language. A map of world languages would look very different. It's worth remembering that of the seven thousand world languages, the majority don't have a unique written alphabet.

Fifty Scripts in
One & Everything

* *Script is written
from right to left*

ᎱᏋᎩᎻᎶ
Adlam *

Հայերէն
Armenian

ꛢꘄꖨꚰꚬ
Bamum

ᜊᜀᜌ᜔
Baybayin (Tagalog)

বাংলা
Bengali

ᝊᝒ
Buhid

ᐃᓄᒃᑎᑐᑦ
Canadian Aboriginal Syllabics (Inuktitut)

𐊀𐊵𐊪𐊭𐊬𐊪𐊴
Carian

𑄞𑄬𑄌
Chakma

ꨌꩌꨆ ꨚ᷆
Cham

ᏣᎳᏆ
Cherokee

𒀭𒐈𒈗𒂍 𒁹
Cuneiform

𐠭𐠍𐠥𐠨
Cypriot *

Egyptian Hieroglyphs *

한글
Hangul

漢字
Hanzi

עברית
Hebrew *

ꦗꦮꦤꦏꦱꦫꦲ
Javanese

ꤚꤢꤟꤢꤡꤢꤢ꤯ ꤢꤢꤢ
Kayah Li

𐨐𐨪𐨯
Kharosthi *

ᨲ᩠ᨿᨴᩢᨾ
Lanna (Tai Tham)

ᰛᰩᰵᰛ
Lepcha

ᤕᤠᤰᤌᤢᤱ(ᤜ)
Limbu

𐀴𐀳𐀢𐀵
Linear B

᭄᭄᭄᭄᭄
Lontara

മലയാളം
Malayalam

ࡌࡍࡃࡀࡉࡀ
*Mandaic **

ꯃꯤꯇꯩ ꯃꯌꯦꯛ
Meitei Mayek

მხედრული
Mkhedruli

မြန်မာဘာသာ
Myanmar

ߒߞߏ
*N'Ko **

قلم النسخ
*Naskh **

ଓଡ଼ିଆ
Odia

᚛᚛ᚋᚌᚐᚑᚒ᚜
Ogham

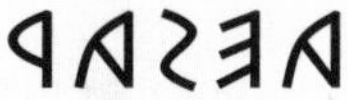

𐌀𐌄𐌑𐌄𐌀
Old Italic

𐒴𐒰𐒵𐒰𐒵𐒲 𐒺𐒰
Osage

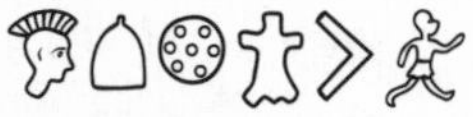

𐇑𐇛𐇜𐇬𐇗𐇚
Phaistos Disk

ꤼꢤꢥ
Rejang

සිංහල
Sinhala

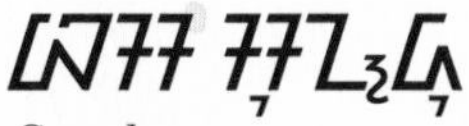

ᮞᮥᮔ᮪ᮓ ᮏᮝ
Sundanese

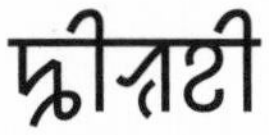

ꠍꠤꠟꠐꠤ
Syloti

ܣܘܪܝܝܐ
*Syriac **

ᝦ᜴ᝲ
Tagbanwa

தமிழ்
Tamil

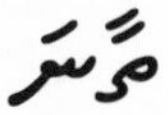

ތާނަ
*Thaana **

ภาษาไทย
Thai

བོད་སྐད།
Tibetan

ⵜⵉⴼⵉⵏⴰⵖ
Tifinagh

ꕙꔤ
Vai

ꆈꌠ
Yi

"It is speakers in whom languages live."

—Mandana Seyfeddinipur | Endangered Languages Archive

ACKNOWLEDGMENTS

Every book is made by many hands, and this one is no exception. So much of what's here wouldn't have come to life without the kind support of the following people:

First, deep gratitude to all the story keepers and creators, especially those working to sustain endangered languages.

Tim Brookes from the Endangered Alphabets Project, who helped write "Some Characters to Be Found in *One & Everything*," offered precious advice, and his feedback has been invaluable.

Mandana Seyfeddinipur from the Endangered Languages Archive was also incredible with her encouragement and support. Thanks as well to the poet Chris McCabe for his own work around endangered poetry and also to the team at Wikitongues for the projects they are running.

Assistance with specific scripts came from many kind people: Naail Abdul Rahman and Aminath Shareehan Ibrahim, founder of the Dhivehi publisher Thakethi, helped with the Dhivehi language script. Thanks to Hassan Hameed for his permission to use the beautiful MV Typewriter font.

Dr. Gareth Owens of Hellenic Mediterranean University was very gracious in answering our questions on the Phaistos Disk. Further reading about his work can be found at daidalika.hmu.gr.

For "Some Characters to Be Found in *One & Everything*," Amalia Gnanadesikan vetted the Thaana, Yumjyi vetted the Tibetan, Marie Thaut vetted the Syloti, and Katherine Forsyth vetted the Ogham. Ahmadou Lamarana Diallo vetted the Adlam, and Abdoulaye Barry was very kind in answering questions on the script. Bill Poser vetted the Canadian Aboriginal Syllabics, and Pia Flamand at Inhabit Media Inc., the first Inuit-owned, independent publishing company in the Canadian Arctic, helped with where to look. Roy Boney vetted the Cherokee. Tiokasin Ghosthorse, founder of the First Voices Indigenous Radio, and Violet Catches, author of *A Giant Teepee in the Sky*, gave very helpful support and advice.

Paul Moreton and Helen Mackenzie Smith were instrumental in getting the project on its feet. Making the art was also no simple task, and without the skill of Josh Attwood, Jess Barton, Gregg Hammerquist, and creative director Ann Stott, these pages would not look the way they do.

The book perhaps would have been unfeasible to produce without the Google Noto fonts project. Thanks also to the artists William Bragg and Oliver Jeffers for their friendship and creative support in its development.

Shona Frazer and Jeff Winston brought much welcome advice to the writing. Lydia Abel's amazing resourcefulness and hard work made the final pages speak with real clarity, and Mona Baloch was invaluable in helping correspond with so many people. Julia Gaviria and Maggie Deslaurier were the excellent copyeditor and proofreader assigned to the project. Thank you also to everyone at Candlewick and Walker Books, the people who bring projects like this into the world.

Heartfelt thanks to Karen Lotz, my editor and publisher. Without her this book would not exist.

Finally, thanks to Haein Song—from conception to completion, you helped with one and everything.